⚓ Pie ⚓

MARCIA VAUGHAN

illustrated by Christine Ross

LEARNING MEDIA®

Distributed in the United States of America by Pacific Learning,
P. O. Box 2723, Huntington Beach, CA 92647-0723
Web site: www.pacificlearning.com

Published 1999 by Learning Media Limited,
Box 3293, Wellington 6001, New Zealand
Web site: www.learningmedia.com

10 9 8 7 6 5 4 3

Printed in Hong Kong

ISBN 0 478 22928 3

PL 9162

Chapter
1

*H*ector Humbug was captain of the *Evil Weevil*. He was the nastiest pirate ever to sail the South Seas. He plundered, and he robbed. He sank ships and cheated at cards, even on Sundays. Captain Humbug disliked *everyone*, especially his cousin Horatio.

Horatio Hogswoggle was captain of the *Bent Barnacle*. He was the meanest pirate ever to sail the North Seas. He plundered, and he robbed. He sank ships and made sweet little grannies walk the plank, even on Sundays. Captain Hogswoggle disliked *everyone*, especially his cousin Hector.

That's why, for twenty years, these two pirate cousins sailed in different seas. That is, until they heard that Peg Leg Lil was sailing her ship, the *Sea Biscuit*, to Shipwreck Island. There she planned to enter the Pirates' Annual Blue-water Bake-off and win first prize with a secret recipe.

"Shiver me timbers!" hooted Captain Humbug. "I'm just the pirate to sink Peg Leg Lil's ship and steal that secret recipe. Hardy har har!" He raised all the sails and turned the *Evil Weevil* to the north.

Many miles away, Captain Hogswoggle yelled, "Scrape the barnacles off me bottom. I'm just the pirate to plunder that recipe and make Peg Leg Lil walk the plank next Sunday. Hody ho ho!" He raised his pirate flag, the Jolly George, and turned the *Bent Barnacle* to the south.

Chapter 2

Now Peg Leg Lil was a true-blue pirate. She could shoot a cannonball through a porthole. She could sail the *Sea Biscuit* safely through a typhoon. She could dig up buried treasure all day long. But there was something about her that nobody knew. Peg Leg Lil was a *terrible* cook. To make things worse, she had no secret recipe for the contest. But, deep in her salty heart, Peg Leg Lil wanted to win first prize in that bake-off more than all the treasure in the world.

So Lil sent the ship's cook up into the crow's-nest and took over the cooking herself.

Every day, while other pirates were robbing and stealing and filling their chests with treasure, Peg Leg Lil was up to her elbows in sugar and shortening and spices.

"Try my barnacle burgers," she told the first mate.

"Try these octopus pancakes," she told the second mate.

"This sea slug soup is really something," she said, spooning some into the bosun's mouth.

"It's really something, all right,"
groaned the bosun. "It's *awful!*"

"*Terrible,*" gagged the first mate.

"*Horrible!*" gurgled the second mate.

And the whole crew abandoned ship.

"Well, I'll be a rusty cutlass," she said. "I'll cook up something delicious for the bake-off, or my name's not Peg Leg Lil!" So she cooked up hard tack hash and fisheye pie.

"Oooh, yuk," she cried. "My crew was right. I *am* an awful, terrible, horrible cook. But I'm stubborn too, and I won't give up," she snorted.

Chapter
3

hrough salty storms and wailing gales, Peg Leg Lil tried to cook a dish so delicious that it would win the bake-off. She was so busy measuring and mixing, stirring and fixing, that she didn't notice two ships sailing into view.

"Ahoy, seadog," cursed Captain Humbug when he saw his cousin Horatio. "This is my patch, and the *Sea Biscuit* is my prize to plunder. Now set sail before I scuttle you. Hardy har har!"

"You blubbering barnacle," Captain Hogswoggle bellowed back. "These are my seas, and Peg Leg Lil's treasure belongs to me. It's you who'd better be off, or I'll blast that bathtub of yours out of the water and swab the deck with your tongue. Hody ho ho!"

Hody ho ho!

"Batten the hatches," hooted Captain Humbug.

"Make fast the rigging," hollered Captain Hogswoggle.

"Load the guns."

"Ready … aim …"

"Fire!"
Both pirates fired.

KERR-BOOM!

The cannonballs soared across the sky in a blaze of blue sparks.

Higher and higher they rose. They rocketed right over the frilly, fringed flag of the *Sea Biscuit*.

Splish.

Splash.

Both pirates missed by a mile.

Chapter 4

*D*own in the kitchen of the *Sea Biscuit*, Peg Leg Lil was madder than a cross-eyed crab.

"Blast those bilge rats!" she stormed as she peered out of the porthole. "All that booming and banging has made my kelp cake fall as flat as a jellyfish. They'll be sorry they ever crossed my path!"

Lil grabbed every ingredient in the galley and leaped up the ladder. She charged across the ship like a cyclone and started stuffing the cannon full of eggs, whipped cream, carrot tops, fish fins, and anything else she could get her floury hands on.

"If you two scurvy sea dogs want my secret recipe so badly, I'll *give* it to you!" she shouted as she lit the fuse and stood back.

Before Hector Humbug and Horatio Hogswoggle could steer clear, the cannon on the deck of the *Sea Biscuit* exploded with a thunderous KERR-BOOM!

Whizz ...
Whap ...
Splat!
The *Evil Weevil* and the *Bent Barnacle* were hit!

Chapter
5

*T*he whirling, swirling mixture sailed through the air and covered both ships from stem to stern in a sticky, mooshy mess.

Hector Humbug tried to cut his way through the slippery slop on his deck.

Horatio Hogswoggle tried to scrape his way across his sticky, soggy ship.

Then a great, gooey gloop of the mixture fell from the mainmast. It landed with a "plop" right across Hector Humbug's face.

He opened his mouth to yell … but instead, a smile spread slowly from ear to ear.

"I'll be a blue-bellied bass! This is the most *delicious* thing I've ever eaten. Hey, Horatio, stop stomping like a stranded sawfish and try a bite."

"I'll be a purple
polka-dotted porpoise
if you're not right," Horatio hooted.
"This is *scrumptious*."

"Hey, Lil, give us your recipe," the two pirates cried.

"Never!" shouted Peg Leg Lil.

"If you'll tell us the recipe, we promise to give up pirating forever and help you open a bakery."

"You mean my recipe is *good?*" she gasped.

"It's not just good," hollered Hector and Horatio. "It's **great!** What do you call it?"

Lil thought for a moment and then laughed, "Why, I call this dish

High-in-the-Sky Pirate Pie."

Chapter 6

*N*ot only did she win first prize in the bake-off, but with the help of Hector and Horatio, Peg Leg Lil opened the first floating bakery on the high seas.

The two cousins worked like whirlwinds in the kitchen while Lil loaded the cannon. Soon the sky was filled with pirate pies. They blasted and boomed them aboard every ship that passed within range.

Word of Peg Leg Lil's incredible edible High-in-the-Sky Pirate Pie traveled as fast as a hurricane. In no time at all, the treasure chests aboard the *Sea Biscuit* were overflowing with gold doubloons.

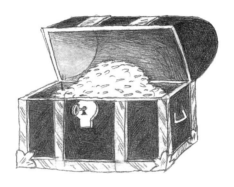

Hector Humbug, Horatio Hogswoggle, and Peg Leg Lil were indeed the happiest, busiest, and *richest* pirates ever to sail the seven seas.